Wheeler's Big Break

Wheeler's

Big Break

by Daniel Schantz

Art by Ned O.

STANDARD PUBLISHING
Cincinnati, Ohio   24-02911

Wheeler's Adventures

Wheeler's Deal

Wheeler's Big Catch

Wheeler's Ghost Town

Wheeler's Good Time

Wheeler's Big Break

Wheeler's Vacation

Wheeler's Freedom

Wheeler's Campaign

Library of Congress Cataloging in Publication Data

Schantz, Daniel.
    Wheeler's big break / by Daniel Schantz ; art by
Ned O.
    p. cm. — (Wheeler's adventures ; 5)
    Summary: Sonny and Earnest Wheeler have a
contest to see which one can repair the most broken
items in one week.
    ISBN 0-87403-451-5 (pbk.)
    [1. Brothers—Fiction. 2. Repairing—Fiction. 3.
Contests—Fiction.] I. Ostendorf, Edward, ill. II.
Title. III. Series: Schantz, Daniel. Wheeler's adven-
tures ; 5.
PZ7.S3338Wb   1988
[Fic]—dc 19   88-9621

Cover illustration by Richard D. Wahl

to my brothers and sisters—
Tom, Mark, Bobby, Gloria, and Linda Joy

Contents

1 • Treasure Chest

A big, dusty spider danced up Sonny's bony arm. It rested on his tattered sleeve just inches from his face, but he never even flinched. His eyes were locked onto a rusty metal box in the trunk of the car. It was a junked car he had found in a gully in the meadow.

A few large drops of rain drummed on the top of the old car, and some angry bees circled his head. "Easy, bees, it's just me." He reached into the trunk with both hands and gripped the sturdy box.

"Oof—this sucker's heavy." He hoisted the box with both arms and swung it out of the trunk. It crashed to the grass with a *ka-whump!* "Wonder what's in it? Maybe it's full of diamonds and rubies. Or rare coins."

With a fist-sized rock he beat at the latches, but the box was rusted shut. He turned the box around and beat on the hinges until his hands were sore. *Plink!* One hinge popped off. Sonny grasped the corner of the lid and pried up. Slowly the lid eased its oyster grip and bent up and off. Eagerly he knelt down over the open box.

"Rags! Old oily rags! Just my luck." The spider leaped off his shoulder and onto the rags. He shooed the insect away and lifted the oily brown rags.

"Well, look at this! tools! And in good shape, too. The rags must have kept them from rusting."

One at a time he fondled the smooth, shiny wrenches and screwdrivers. He laid them out neatly on the grass beside him.

"These would cost a fortune." He glanced across the meadow to his house. "I gotta show these to Dad."

Sonny tied the old rags together, laid the tools on them and rolled them up together. Stuffing the heavy package under his arm, he swished and skipped through the tall meadow grasses toward home.

Soon the sturdy blue house with white shutters loomed just across Morley Highway. Sonny slapped the *Mulberry City Limit* sign as he passed it. He scurried across the road to the used car lot next to his house, where his father was working on a car.

Sonny dropped the heavy tools on the gravel at his father's feet and spread them out for him to admire, but Mr. Wheeler was deep in thought. The car engine rumbled and gurgled as he studied it. With a piece of garden hose held to his ear, he probed the engine with the other end, like a doctor using his stethoscope. At last he laid the hose aside, shook his head, and wiped his hands on a rag. Then he noticed Sonny.

"Oh, hi, Sonny. Where you been all morning?"

Sonny pointed at the tools on the ground. Mr. Wheeler knelt over them. "Hey, nice tools. Been hitting the rummage sales again?"

"Nope. Guess again."

"I give up."

Sonny pointed to the meadow that sloped down to Long Branch Lake. "Out there. In the trunk of an old junker. An old Plymouth in the gully."

Mr. Wheeler shook his head and smiled. "Sonny, sometimes your luck amazes me." Soon his face turned back to the car he was working on. He stroked his dark mustache and mumbled, "I just wish I had some of your kind of luck with this engine."

"What's wrong with it?" Sonny asked, wide-eyed. He leaned on the fender and peered under the hood.

"Just listen to it. Hear that? It's missing."

"Plugs?" Sonny asked.

"Naw. I put in new ones. I checked everything twice. I just can't understand this machine."

At that moment, Sonny's brother Earnest moseyed over to the car, rolling up the crisp sleeves of his pink shirt as he drew near. A big book was tucked under his left arm.

"What's up, you guys?"

Sonny sneered at his short, well-dressed brother. "Nothing *you* would understand, that's for sure. You know, I'll bet you're the only person in the world who can walk to the library without getting a grain o' dust on his shoes." He kicked some gravel towards Earnest's shoes.

"Quit it!" Earnest warned. Then he peered at

the troubled engine. He was careful not to touch anything greasy. For a moment he just listened and watched with darting eyes, hoping to spot the trouble.

"There's your problem," he said smugly. He pointed to the air cleaner on top of the engine. "You got that nut on too tight."

Sonny grinned at his father, and his father grinned back. "Right, Earnest. Listen, you're the only nut around here that's too tight."

Mr. Wheeler chuckled to himself.

"Oh, yeah?" Earnest snapped back. He reached out and loosened the wing nut on the air cleaner. Instantly the engine smoothed out.

"Well I'll be . . ." Mr. Wheeler mumbled. "He's right. That nut was warping the gasket here, letting in too much air."

Sonny turned purple in the face. "And you say *I'm* lucky, Dad? Earnest doesn't know a muffler from an ashtray, and he fixes an engine with two clean fingers!"

Earnest wiped his fingers with his hanky. "I can fix anything you can fix, Sonny."

"Awww, get outta here, Earnest. Go play on the freeway. You couldn't pour water out of a boot if the instructions were on the heel."

"Hey, you're just jealous 'cause I beat you at your own game."

"Jealous? How could I ever be jealous of someone who wears pink dress shirts? You know, you would make a terrific girl. You even smell good."

Earnest turned the same shade as his shirt.

"All right, you guys," Mr. Wheeler warned. "Cool your engines. If you have to prove something, why don't you see which one of you can fix that garage door?"

"What's wrong with it?"

"I'll show you." Mr. Wheeler pulled a small black box from his pocket and thumbed a button on top of it. The garage door started moving up, then stopped cold at the halfway point. "See, it's been that way for a month."

Sonny glared at Earnest. "I can fix it before you can."

"Big deal," Earnest replied. He started to walk away.

Mr. Wheeler slammed down the hood of his car. "Tell you what, guys. If one of you can fix that door, I'll pay you what a repairman might charge."

Earnest stopped in his tracks. "How much is that?"

"Oh, I 'spect, well . . . at least fifty bucks."

Sonny's eyes began to glow money green. Without another word he scooped up his new tools and sprinted to the garage door. Earnest came flying behind him.

At bedtime the two of them were still working on the garage door.

2 • In a Fix

The next morning Sonny and his mother were sitting at the kitchen table. Mrs. Wheeler's tall, slender body was hunched over her plate of scrambled eggs. Sonny was almost finished with breakfast when Earnest strode into the kitchen with a piece of paper in his hand. He spread the sheet out on the table in front of Sonny.

"What's this?" Sonny wanted to know. He was slurping an orange slice.

"Read it," Earnest ordered him.

Sonny dribbled juice on the paper as he read it.

"Oh, it's another one of your stupid contracts. Why don't you just tell me what it says?"

"Okay." He held it up and read it smartly. "It says, whoever fixes the most things and the hardest things is the winner."

"Winner of what?" Sonny butted in.

"I'm getting to that. Cool your jets."

Mr. Wheeler shuffled into the kitchen and popped some bread in the toaster. "Ohhhh," he moaned. "What a night! That bed has got to go."

"What's wrong with the bed?" Sonny asked.

"What's wrong with it? It sounds like it's ready to die. Every time I roll over, it creaks and pops like a corncrib in a windstorm."

Sonny and Earnest giggled.

"And the springs squeak like a cage full of hungry hamsters."

"Well, Ralph, we've had that bed since we got married." Mrs. Wheeler said. "That's twenty years ago."

"And what did you put under the sheets, anyhow?"

"Just a plastic mattress cover."

"For what? I haven't wet the bed since I was three. It sounds like I'm sleeping on a big package of corn chips."

Earnest smiled, then went on reading. "Okay, where was I? Oh yes—if I win, I get that set of encyclopedias you won't sell me because you are so stinkin' selfish, even though you never read 'em yourself and just use them to make your room look good."

"And if I win?" Sonny asked with a belch.

"You aren't going to win, so it doesn't really matter."

Sonny stiffened. "If I win, I get to use your computer which you are selfish with and just use to show off and don't really even know how to work it right yet. I get to use it a whole month, without even asking."

Earnest winced. "My computer? But . . ."

"Take it or leave it."

With a pained look, Earnest scribbled "Computer" into the contract.

"Who's gonna judge this contest?" Sonny asked.

Earnest went on reading. "Each person must keep a written record of every repair job. Mom and Dad will be the final judges. The contest closes Saturday noon." He paused and added, "Spring break is over Monday."

"Okay, I can live with that. Where do I sign?"

Sonny scratched his name on the line and then

excused himself. He pointed his lanky body toward the door and break-danced out of the house, singing, "Shoo be doo wa doo, Sonny gonna fix it for you."

"I'm going to the library," Earnest announced, and he headed to his room for a clean shirt.

"And I'm going to the shop," Mr. Wheeler added.

"I'll be out to the office as soon as I stack these dishes," Mrs. Wheeler called after him.

In a few minutes Sonny stumbled back into the empty house, lugging an old shopping bag full of his tools and other equipment he would need for fixing things. He went straight to his parents' bedroom.

Sonny dropped his shopping bag and studied the unmade bed. Then he climbed on it and bounced up and down a few times.

"Well, the springs need oil, that's for sure." He threw the covers off to one corner of the room, then lifted the mattress up and leaned it against the wall. The springs were much heavier, and he groaned as he hoisted them up and leaned them against the mattress.

"Whew! What a mess!" Dust flew in his face and he sputtered it away. From the shopping bag he pulled a can of spray oil and glanced at the label. "Spray Lube. Stops squeaks, cleans, and protects."

He tested the spray in the air, then carefully aimed it at one bed spring. Then another. One by one he soaked the springs with the wet spray.

"Ugh! Stuff smells like a trash can on a hot day."

At last the can was empty and he tossed it into the wastebasket with a *clank.*

"Now I gotta do something about these corner joints." He sat on the floor and jiggled a corner joint to see how bad it creaked.

"Ah-hah. I know just what I need." He bounded off to the bathroom and back in ten seconds flat. In his hand was a mushy bar of soap.

"Ta tummmm," he sang to himself as he unfastened each joint and smeared it with soap, then refastened it.

He was on the last joint when something went wrong.

"Uh-oh." One of the joints dropped apart and hit the floor with a *bang.* When he grabbed for it, another joint broke loose.

"Whoaaaa!" he yelled, but it was too late. The other joints also came apart with a *thud, bang, bump, clunk!* Then the cross pieces fell apart.

"Help!" he hollered. Suddenly the heavy headboard came crashing down on his head, followed by the springs, then the mattress. Then everything grew very quiet.

There he lay under a pile of lumber, moaning and groaning with pain.

All at once Cherry, a neighbor girl, appeared in the doorway. "Sonny! What happened? Are you okay?"

Sonny peeked out from under a board. "Cherry? Where did you come from?"

"The door was open," she explained. "I heard you yelling."

Sonny staggered to his feet and dusted his clothes.

"Ohhhh, I think I'm dead. Look, Cherry, you got to promise not to tell anyone what you just saw. Ohhh, my poor achin' body."

With Cherry's help, Sonny finally got the bed back together, but it kept wanting to fall apart.

"Guess I got the joints too slippery," he mumbled. He wandered around the house and returned with a big roll of cellophane tape.

Cherry held the tape holder while Sonny wrapped each joint with long pieces of the sticky plastic. Then he made the bed and stood back to

admire his work. He popped a fresh toothpick in his mouth and smiled a great smile. "Hey, hey! Not bad, not bad." He pushed on the mattress to test it. "Not a squeak in your sleep, Zeke." From his back pocket he pried a small notebook. On the first page he scribbled, "April 3, fixed one full-sized bed like new."

"Whatcha all of a sudden fixing things for?" Cherry asked.

Sonny just hummed and smiled to himself. "Tell you later, after I sweep up this dust."

While Sonny was working on the bed, Earnest was exploring the Mulberry library for ideas.

"You got anything about how to fix stuff?" he asked the new, young librarian.

"Fix stuff?"

"You know, like fixing chairs and sweepers and radios, things like that?" He looked at her strangely and added, "You're new here, aren't you?"

She put down the book she was reading and motioned for him to follow her. "Yes, this is my first day." She pointed him to a section of the library and then returned to her seat.

Earnest talked to himself as he sorted through the big books. His eyes were bright with excitement, and his hands trembled as he thumbed through the books rapidly. "Yo! Look at all these books. Sonny doesn't have a chance when I get this stuff under my belt."

He began toting stacks of books to the counter, five at a time, until the counter was piled high. So high the librarian was hidden behind the stacks.

Finally he was done. He peeked around the stacks and said, "I'm ready for checkout."

The librarian smiled and reached for her rubber stamp. "Hummm, we have a little problem here, young man. Some of these are reference books. They can't be checked out."

Earnest looked irritated. The lady set some of the books off to the side. The stacks were shrinking fast. Then the lady stopped again.

"Oops, we have another little problem." She pointed to a sign on the wall by the pencil sharpener. "You aren't allowed to check out more than three books on any one topic." She set aside some more books.

Earnest tugged at his collar and looked around impatiently. The stack had dwindled to three books—two on fixing furniture and one on fixing lamps.

The librarian stamped the books, then turned to look at a small card file. "Just a moment, I need to check the file of overdue books." She frowned. "I'm sorry, young man, but you have two overdue books. I can't let you check out any books at all until these are returned and the fines paid."

Earnest turned a deep red in the face, and he scowled at the lady. "What? No books at all? I thought this was a library! I thought you *liked* for people to read books! Did I get in a museum by mistake? Look, I'll bring the overdue books in later today. Promise."

The librarian's lips tightened and she shook her head. "Sorry. No deal. The rules, you know."

Earnest tromped back and forth, returning the books to the shelves and grumbling to himself. "There's gotta be a way to get these books. I can't win without good ideas." Suddenly he stopped and smiled at the librarian. "Uh . . . is Mrs. Grace, the head librarian, in today?"

The lady nodded. "Upstairs, I think."

Earnest bounded up the steps. In a few minutes he came back down, trailing behind Mrs. Grace.

Ten minutes later he left the library with his backpack full of books and nine more stacked in his arms.

He chuckled to himself. "It pays to go right to the top."

3 • Bedlam

Earnest staggered in the door at lunchtime and dropped into the nearest kitchen chair with a moan.

Mrs. Wheeler snatched some sandwiches from the microwave and plunked them down on the counter. "What's in the backpack, Earnest?"

Earnest stacked an armload of books on the table, then slung his backpack to the floor. "More of *these*," he said.

"Books?"

"Not just books. These are *official* repair manuals. I had to get special permission to check them out."

"Repair manuals?"

"Yep. You'd have thought I was checking out the Constitution of the United States, the way they carried on. I had to sign papers, make promises . . . for a while I thought they were going to fingerprint me and take a blood sample."

Mrs. Wheeler smiled as she set the table. "And what are you going to do with all these repair manuals?"

Earnest wriggled a piece of paper from an old notebook and pinned it to the kitchen bulletin board. "It's a contest. Sonny and I have a dare to see who can fix the most broken things." With a bold red marker he printed the word REPAIRS at the top of the paper.

"This is where I need your help, Mom. Anything you know of that's broken, write it up here, and we'll fix it."

Mrs. Wheeler untied her apron and hung it up. "You can write up 'vacuum cleaner' for starters. Something is stuck in the hose, and the cord won't retract."

After lunch Earnest sprawled out on the living room floor, framed by a pile of open repair man-

uals. He started with a book on home appliances, flipping to the section on vacuum cleaners.

By late afternoon he closed the books and laid his head on the floor to rest.

Mrs. Wheeler strolled into the room with a glass of cola for him. "What's wrong, Earnest? You look beat."

Earnest threw up his hands. "It's these books. Everything is so rotten complicated. It's not fair. Sonny can fix things so easy. It comes natural to him." He chugged the cola.

"So you think you might have bitten into a monster?"

"Yeah, I guess. I'm a little clutzy with my hands. But Mom, I *gotta* win this contest. I want those encyclopedias so bad I could eat bugs."

"I'll bet that's not the only reason you want to win," she replied. She had a twinkle in her eye as she took the empty glass from him.

Earnest grinned sheepishly. "Yeah. Don't you worry, I'll beat him one way or another."

Mrs. Wheeler ambled back to the kitchen and Earnest stacked his books in the corner. "There's got to be an easier way to beat Sonny," he mumbled to himself. "There's just *got* to be."

For a while he sat on the floor thinking. Suddenly he stopped thinking and began glowing. "Yeah, that's it! Why didn't I think of that before?" He leaped up with an armload of books and stumbled to his room.

It was almost eleven that night before everyone was in bed. When Earnest was sure everyone was dressed for sleep, he quietly pried up his bedroom window and lowered himself to the ground. In one hand he carried a flashlight and in the other a set of keys to the office. Working quietly, he opened the garage office door and slid inside. He went straight to the computer and turned it on. In the dark room the computer seemed as bright as a searchlight, so he covered it with his arms as he worked.

Meanwhile, Sonny was just dozing off when he heard a commotion in his parents' bedroom. "They've probably noticed the bed doesn't squeak," he said to himself. "I'll bet I get an award for this. Mom will probably fix me a pizza every night for a week."

His thoughts were interrupted by the dark shadow of his father in the doorway. "Sonny!" his father bellowed. "Do you know anything about this?" He held up the empty can of spray oil for Sonny to see.

Sonny stiffened. "Uh, well—yeah, I guess so."

Mr. Wheeler grabbed Sonny by the forearm and guided him firmly up the stairs to their bedroom.

"What's wrong?" Sonny muttered over and over.

Mr. Wheeler stood Sonny in the doorway to their bedroom. "Take a deep breath and I think you can figure out what's wrong."

Sonny sniffed the air, then coughed twice. "Kinda strong, isn't it?"

"Strong?" his father roared. "It's a *gas chamber*. We could be dead by morning!"

"But I *fixed* it," Sonny protested. "The squeaks are gone."

His father grabbed Sonny by the head with both hands and peered into his right ear. "Your brains are gone too." Then he moved the bed partly aside with his foot. "The squeaks are gone all right. But look at this!" Puddles of oil lay all over the floor under the bed. He shoved the spray can in Sonny's face. "See this? It says, 'Use with adequate ventilation.'"

He stared at Sonny like an angry wrestler. "You and I are going to have a nice long talk in the morning."

Meanwhile, Mrs. Wheeler was opening the

windows of the bedroom. Then she began mopping up the oil spots with tissues.

"I'll help," Sonny said quietly. Mr. Wheeler stuck a thick, strong finger in Sonny's face. "You get out of here and get to bed. Your kind of help we don't need."

Sonny shuffled downstairs and crawled into bed. He lay there thinking about what he would say to his father in the morning.

All at once the ceiling shook violently and a crashing sound made him jump right off his bed. "What the . . ."

Sonny sprinted out of the room and streaked up the stairs. When he slid to a stop he saw his father sitting on the edge of the mattress, which was lying on the floor. With one hand his father was prying the headboard off Mrs. Wheeler. Cellophane tape was wrapped around his other hand, and a look of despair was on his face.

Sonny turned and fled to his room and locked the door.

4 • Dirty Tricks

Sonny opened his eyes and squinted at the clock. "Hmmm. It's only eight. Maybe if I don't get up till ten, Dad will forget about last night." He rolled over and went back to sleep.

At ten-fifteen Sonny tiptoed into the kitchen. It was empty.

Very quietly he opened a box of chocolate chip granola bars. One he stuffed in his mouth and another in his shirt pocket. "Maybe I can sneak away to the park and live on berries and nuts till this blows over."

The kitchen door swung open and Mrs. Wheeler stepped in smartly. "Sonny?"

Sonny raised his hands. "Don't shoot!"

She crossed her arms and studied him with beady eyes. Then she motioned toward the garage. "Your father wants to see you out in the car lot."

"Ohhhhhh," he groaned. "Listen, Mom, if I don't come back, call an ambulance. No, call the *morgue*."

She winked at him as he trudged out the door, but she was not smiling.

Mr. Wheeler was stacking old tires beside the garage. His dark hair was damp with sweat and his face was smudged with grease. When he saw Sonny, he stopped and stared at him, thinking about what he was going to say. Sonny stopped about fifteen feet away, mangling the toothpick he carried between his lips. "You wanted to see me, Dad?" His voice quivered.

Mr. Wheeler motioned for Sonny to follow and tromped out into the car lot. He stopped by a bright red used car and patted it on the fender. "Nice car, huh?" he said to Sonny.

Sonny looked suspicious, then nodded.

Mr. Wheeler went on. "Yes sir, sure looks like a

nice car." He peered in the driver's window. "Only 20,000 miles on it too."

"Really?" Sonny replied, his voice still shaky.

"Yep. You know, Sonny, I've been fixing cars and selling them for twenty years. You would think I'd know better than to buy a car like this at an auction."

"What do you mean? Is something wrong with it? It looks great."

"You bet it does. But this car is worth about ten cents. Not only worthless, it could be downright dangerous." He opened the driver's door and pointed to some oil change stickers on the door frame. "See this? Oil was changed at 88,000 miles."

Sonny's eyes grew large. "What does that mean?"

"It means the speedometer has turned over. This car has 120,000 miles on it, not 20,000."

Mr. Wheeler reached in and snapped off the rubber brake pedal pad. "See this? Brand new. Somebody was trying to hide the wear and tear that always shows up on the pedals." Next he squatted down in front of the car. "Look at this. The front and back wheels are not in line with each other. This car has been in a wreck." He stood up and pulled a small magnet from his pocket and touched it to the side of the car. "Bet there's been a lot of body work done to hide the damage." He touched the magnet all along the side of the car. "See? This is all fiberglass—this whole side of the car has been puttied. The magnet doesn't grab fiberglass." He took hold of the door handle and began rapidly opening and closing the door. "See this? The door doesn't close square. It's been wrecked, all right."

Sonny rubbed his fingers along the door edge. "Yeah, I see."

"There's more here, Sonny." He grabbed a white cardboard *Sale* sign from the windshield and laid it on the ground under the engine. Then he went to the back of the car, stooped down, and rubbed the inside of the tail pipe with his finger. He held it up to Sonny's nose. "Smell this? It's oil. This car's burning oil like a kerosene lantern."

Sonny shook his head in disbelief. "Well, at least the tires are good," he said.

Mr. Wheeler took out his pocketknife and scraped the side of a tire, then held the blade to Sonny's face. "Know what this is? It's black paint. These tires have been painted to look new." He kicked one of them. "Retreads, too." Next he pushed hard on the back bumper with his foot, and the car rocked up and down like a boat in a storm. "Springs and shocks are completely gone." He stepped briskly around to the front of the car and pulled the white sign from under the engine. "Look at this, Sonny, can you believe it?" He held the card where Sonny could see several drops of fluid on the card. He dipped a finger in one and sniffed it. "This is motor oil. Bearings are leaking." He sniffed another one. "Power steering fluid." He rubbed a finger through the third spot, sniffed it and shook his head. "Brake fluid." He pulled a rag from his pocket and wiped his hands. "So what we have here, Sonny, is an accident looking for a place to happen."

Then he paused and stared into Sonny's eyes. He put his hands on Sonny's shoulders. "Sonny, do you understand why I've shown you this car? I mean, in your own words, what am I trying to say to you?"

Sonny hung his head and rubbed the toes of his shoes together. "I guess . . . I guess you're trying to tell me not to put a bed together with Scotch tape?"

Mr. Wheeler's serious look changed to a wide, happy smile. "Well, you're a lot smarter than you look. Hey, listen. I'm glad you boys are into fixing things, but let's fix 'em right, okay?"

"Then you're not mad?" Sonny asked.

"Last night I was mad enough to spit razor blades, but not now." He looked around, then lowered his voice to a whisper. "To tell you the truth, I've been looking for a good excuse to get rid of that old bed. Want to get one of those king-sized jobs that holds four pillows, you know?" He punched Sonny gently on the shoulder and chuckled.

Sonny grinned with relief, then turned to leave.

"How are you boys doing on that garage door? I sure would hate to give that fifty dollars to some stranger."

Sonny shrugged and shook his head.

In the afternoon the Wheelers went shopping, all except Earnest. Earnest kept eyeing the broken garage door. "That shouldn't be so hard to fix," he said to himself. "If I could get the fifty dollars I could buy my own new encyclopedias." He wandered out into his father's shop and picked out some tools. He found a fresh, blue denim apron and added it to his armload of tools and repair books. He laid everything out neatly in front of the stubborn garage door.

He tied on the apron, then picked up the remote button. For a while he worked the door up and down, trying to see why it wouldn't go all the way to the top. He found nothing, so he laid the button down on the driveway and picked up a book on household repairs. He sat with his back to the door and thumbed through the book until he found a section on "garage doors."

"Hmmm, this doesn't seem too hard. The wheels are pulled up the track by the chain until it reaches the top. Then the switch reverses. It must be something in the track."

He shifted to a more comfortable position and set the book down. The book plopped right on the remote button. With no warning the door hummed and jerked upward. The door handle caught in the strings of his apron, and Earnest rose into the air.

"Yo! What the . . . hey, I'm caught . . . how in the . . ." Now he was dangling in midair like a worm on a fishhook. He started to yell for help, then stopped. "I can't let anyone see me like this." He twisted and turned, trying to free himself.

"This is crazy. What am I doing up here?" He tried to reach the button with his hand, then with his foot, but it was just a little too far away. "I've got to get off this before someone sees me." He looked around for some kind of help. "If I untie this apron I'll land right on my kisser." The door handle was cutting into his back, and he let out a little moan.

"I can't believe this is happening to me." He glanced at his watch. "Mom and Dad will be back any minute. No way am I gonna be up here when they get here."

He slipped off his left shoe and aimed it at the button. It glanced off the book, but it moved the book out of the way. He held his breath and dropped his other shoe right over the button. The heel hit the button, but it moved him up a couple inches higher, not down.

"Arrgghhh! What am I donna do?" Suddenly he saw his parents' pickup truck in the distance.

"Uh-oh." With a desperate lunge he tried to twist free, planning to fall to the ground, even if it killed him. But he only got more tangled in the handle. On his face was a look of horror as the truck got closer.

"If I can't go down, I'll just go up," he said bravely. With a mighty groan he heaved himself up and grabbed for the wooden molding of the door frame. "Got it!" He clung tightly with one

hand while he untied the apron with his other hand. The apron broke loose and dangled from his neck loosely. Now he grabbed the molding with both hands. Breathing hard, he walked himself across the molding with his fingertips, then dropped to a pile of old tires at the corner.

When the truck arrived, Earnest was sitting on an old tire, his shoes on, calmly reading a book.

5 • It's Magic

Sonny and Earnest were wrestling in the yard, running, tagging, and falling like two puppies. Inside the office, Mrs. Wheeler frowned at the computer screen. Her fingers played the keys like an expert organist, and the screen shone green on her troubled face. But no matter what she did, the screen would not respond. It just seemed frozen solid. She shook her head and twisted her lips with disgust.

The tapping of the keys was joined by the tap of April rain on the window. Moments later an umbrella passed by the window and someone rapped on the door.

Mrs. Wheeler slapped the computer on its side and leaned back in her creaky chair. "Come in!" she said. Her voice was tinged with anger.

The door slowly opened and Cherry wiggled in behind a red watermelon umbrella. She was wearing a matching red dress with black seeds printed on it, and shiny black boots.

The sight of Cherry made Mrs. Wheeler calm down for a moment. "Hi, Cherry. My, you certainly look good enough to eat."

Cherry blushed. "I like watermelons," she said, folding up the umbrella.

"Me too."

"Are you okay, Mrs. Wheeler? You sound kind of upset."

"You've got a good ear, Cherish Elizabeth. Oh, it's this computer. It was working fine yesterday, but now . . . well, that's my problem. What brings you out in the rain?"

"I . . . I wanted to ask you a favor." She stood the umbrella in a corner and sat down on a wooden box. "See, I like to grow things, you know, like flowers and stuff."

"So I've noticed."

"And, well . . . not to hurt your feelings, but well, I don't know how to ask."

"Ask me for the moon."

Cherry took a deep breath. "Okay. I was wondering if it would be okay if I took care of your flowers and bushes and things around the house?"

"Oh, Cherry, you don't even need to ask. I would be thrilled. I will *pay* you to care for them. I hate yard work and I've neglected everything. It's worse than ironing, and I loathe ironing."

"I don't want any pay," Cherry said, shaking her head. She picked up her umbrella to leave. "I just like to do it for fun. And I'm real sorry about your computer."

Mrs. Wheeler glanced at the glowing screen. "Me too. Ralph is gonna have kittens when he finds out."

Cherry left and Mrs. Wheeler walked slowly to the garage, where her husband was washing car parts.

"Ralph? We've got big troubles."

He looked up and blinked. "The boys again?"

"Nope. Worse. The computer—it's broken."

Mr. Wheeler rolled his eyes. "Oh, great, just great. Just what I need to make my life complete!"

Sonny and Earnest fell into the garage, wrestling each other to the floor. Mr. Wheeler glared at them. "You two fight somewhere else or I'll take you both down, and I mean it."

Sonny jumped up and looked at his mother. "Who crimped *his* hose?"

"It's the computer, boys. It's on the fritz."

Earnest staggered to his feet. "Maybe I can fix it. Sometimes I can fix my own." He strode confidently toward the office door, followed by the others.

"You'll probably make it worse," Sonny argued. "Probably blow up the office, the whole town, maybe even the world."

Earnest hunched over the machine and fiddled with the keys, then removed the disk.

"Just be careful, Earnest."

"If you can fix this, Earnest, I will be your servant for the rest of my life. When this thing goes, my business goes with it."

Earnest tapped more keys, wiggled parts, and juggled the cords, humming to himself as he worked. "Ah, here we go," he said smugly. disconnecting the keyboard and blowing on the connections. No one but Earnest noticed a tiny piece of paper flutter to the ground. Earnest plugged the wire in again, then slid a disk into the drive and booted it. The screen flickered to life, and he punched a few keys.

"Hey, it's working! It's magic!" Mrs. Wheeler squealed. She tried to hug him, but he wriggled free.

"You're a genius," Mr. Wheeler added. "If I had to take that to the shop I would lose at least two weeks' work."

Earnest stood up and looked at Sonny as if to say, "Beat that, big brother."

The boys wrestled their way out of the office. The rain was over for the moment. They spotted Cherry pulling some weeds from around the lilac bushes.

"Hi, watermelon," Sonny said.

"You look a little seedy," Earnest added. "Got anything that needs fixin'? Sonny and I are the number one and two fixer-uppers."

"I know," she replied. "Sonny told me about your contest." She shook damp grass from hands, then wiped them on her dress. "I think my grandma has a radio that's broken . . . and my bike is acting kinda funny. The brakes squeak."

"Needs oil," Sonny snapped back.

"Does not," Earnest contradicted him. "Just needs cleaning. Bring it to me if you want it fixed right. Sonny thinks oil cures everything."

Cherry covered her mouth with her hand and giggled. "Or Scotch tape," she added.

Sonny hung his head and muttered to himself.

Cherry turned and winked at Earnest. "Earnest," she said, "how are you coming with that garage door?" She was grinning, and her voice had a teasing tone to it.

"Garage door?" Earnest asked, sounding surprised. "Oh, I've kinda given up on that."

Cherry was still grinning. "Afraid of heights?" she teased.

A look of horror came to his face. He pulled her aside and whispered in her ear. "Do you mean you *saw* me?"

She nodded and giggled. "I wish I had a camera."

Earnest shook a finger in her face. "If you want to go on living, you better forget what you saw. You got it?" He made a slashing sign at his throat to warn her.

"What are you guys up to?" Sonny hollered at them. "I hate secrets."

"Nothing," Cherry and Earnest said in unison.

6 • Shut-Eye

On Thursday morning, Sonny was singing to himself as he headed for his bedroom. The singing stopped abruptly when he entered the doorway.

"Earnest! What are you doing in my room?" A clap of thunder outside accented his words, like a voice from Heaven.

Earnest was lounging on the bed, surrounded by books. "Awww, keep your pants on, I was just looking at your 'cylopedias."

"Well, you can just *un*-look, because they aren't yours and never will be and just get your slimy, grimy claws off of 'em before they get messed up or I'll mess you up."

Earnest pinched a notebook from his pocket and snapped it open. "You're just mad 'cause I'm beating you. Let's see, I fixed the vacuum cleaner, the kitchen chair, and the computer. I'll get *big* points for the computer, you can count on that."

Sonny looked at his own notebook and frowned. Without a word he stuffed it back in his pocket.

"You'll get points *off* for messing up that bed," Earnest predicted.

Mrs. Wheeler appeared in the doorway with two large baskets of laundry. "Which one of you wants to carry these to the basement for me? My knees are giving out again."

Earnest pointed at Sonny, and Sonny pointed at Earnest. "He does," they said in unison.

"Earnest, I think it's your turn."

Earnest dragged himself off the bed and strained at the heavy baskets. When he reached the bottom of the basement stairs he dropped the baskets with a *whump*. Just then the sump pump kicked on, startling him with its whining, grinding noise. He watched the pump slurping water out of the leaky basement. Then he began to fiddle with the pump.

A few minutes later he headed back up the steps. As he passed by the basement window he flinched. Cherry was watching him, staring at him strangely. His face turned red. He gave a weak wave, then hurried on up the stairs.

Sonny was sitting at the kitchen table, sorting through a pile of his mother's jewelry. Earnest sneered as he passed by. "Fixin' jewelry? How sweet. Be sure to try it on when you're done. You'll be real purty in pearls." He swaggered out the door and called back, "Me, I'm going to fix Cherry's bike—a man's job."

Sonny threw a rag at Earnest, then went back to his project. In a few minutes he fixed several bracelets and necklaces. Then he started to work on earrings.

"Hmmmmm. These will have to be glued." He scrounged through the kitchen drawer for a tube of glue. "Ah, here we go. Super Glue. One drop lifts a jeep. I've seen this stuff on TV."

Working slowly, he glued the broken ear clamps back to their settings. The glue dried instantly, and soon he was about done.

"Phew! This stuff stinks worse than a skunk's armpit."

He rubbed his nose. "Makes my eyes water." He

rubbed his left eye. "Ouch! That stuff burns!"
Suddenly he set up straight. "Hey! My eye! What
the . . . Help! My eye, I glued my eye shut!" He
leaped up and ran to the bathroom, shouting, "My
eye, my eye! I'm blind, I'm blind!"

Mrs. Wheeler came running, her face white
with concern. "What's wrong, Sonny? What is
it?"

"My eye, my eye! I glued my eye shut. Ohhh, it
hurts."

Mrs. Wheeler grabbed him by the jaw and studied his eye closely. Tears dribbled from the sealed
eye and streaked down his cheek. "Hold still. It
looks like you've just glued your eyelashes together. Stand right there, I've got some remover in
the drawer."

She was back in seconds. With a tissue she
wiped his eyelashes. "Now try it."

Sonny blinked, then his eye opened all the way.
"It's open! I can see! I'm not blind!" Then a serious look came over him. "Mom, listen to me. If
you tell Earnest about this, so help me I will run
away from home and never come back."

Her eyes twinkled. "What's it worth to you?"

"Mom! I'm not fooling. You do and I'll . . ."

"Relax, your secret's safe. To tell the truth, I

once glued my lips shut with that stuff. Your father found it very amusing. That's why I had the remover on hand."

Sonny moped outside, blinking over and over again. He found Earnest fixing Cherry's bike. He was wearing one of his mother's flowered aprons and a pair of white garden gloves.

"Oh, I see you're doing a man's work," he teased. "In a woman's apron and pretty white gloves. You look so sweet. Be careful or you might get a nasty smudge on your smooth white skin."

Earnest blushed. "I get the job done, that's what counts."

"Well, *I'm* ahead of you," Sonny boasted. "I just fixed sixteen pieces of jewelry, and jewelry is close to Mom's heart. She will put me right over the top. I'll probably make the cover of LIFE Magazine."

Earnest made grumbling noises and jerked on the brake cable.

"I'm gonna try another idea on that garage door," Sonny said. Then he reached for a greasy washer and smeared it on Earnest's cheek and dashed away.

"Hey! Get outta here!"

When Earnest had Cherry's bike fixed, he

leaned it against the porch railing. Then he wiped his hands on a rag and looked around nervously.

Trying to look casual, he strolled to the side yard and opened the door of the garden shed. Again he looked all around. Then he slipped into the shed and pulled the door tight behind him.

Nearby Cherry was planting some lily bulbs. When she heard the shed door close, she swirled around and stared at the shed. She listened to strange noises leaking from the door crack. She set down her trowel. She tiptoed to the shed and stopped to listen. She peeked through the door crack and watched Earnest messing with the lawn mower. Then she swung open the door.

The flood of light from the doorway startled Earnest. He jerked, like a bug under a freshly-turned stone. Then he saw Cherry standing in the doorway.

"Whatcha doin'?" she asked.

"Oh, uh, me? What am I doin'? You mean here? Uh, well . . ." His voice cracked and his hands looked like they didn't know where to go. "Uh, I'm just . . . just checking over this mower. Yeah, that's it. Just trying to keep everything in good shape around here, you know?" He picked up a rag and pretended to polish the mower.

Cherry looked at him with questions in her wise eyes. "Oh," she said, meekly. She turned to leave, then looked back.

Earnest gave a weak smile and an even weaker wave. "See ya," he said. Cherry nodded and went back to her work.

Earnest closed the shed door and trotted to the office.

7 • The Lock-In

On Thursday afternoon, Earnest peered at the bulletin board for new things to fix. On the cover of his notebook he printed, "Typewriter key is stuck, toilet seat loose, cabinet drawer sticking, floor fan squeaks." He read over the list again, then scratched out the words "toilet seat." He said to himself, "Sonny can have that one." He strolled down the hall to his room.

Sonny was typing on Earnest's computer when Earnest arrived. Earnest took one look and stiffened. His face turned steel gray.

"What are you doing?" he shouted at Sonny. "Get away from my computer!" Sonny pretended not to hear. *"Did you hear me? Get your maggot fingers off my keyboard!"*

Sonny just kept typing. "You were messin' with my books, so I'm messin' with your toys."

Earnest hit a couple of keys and the computer blanked out. "It's not a toy. It's a real machine, and you get away from it," he warned, nose-to-nose with Sonny. "What's wrong with your eye?" he added, and reached out to touch it.

Sonny swatted Earnest's hand away. "Nothin's wrong with my eye, unless it's from looking at your face." He pushed away from the computer and moped to the door.

"Aw, go fix the toilet seat," said Earnest. "I saved that job just for you."

"What a guy! How can I ever thank you?" Sonny said, a barb in his voice. "I think I will. Wouldn't want you to get a germ on your sterilized body."

In a few minutes Sonny had tightened the loose toilet seat, then he sat on the floor playing with his new tools. As he started to leave, he noticed the bathroom door lock was sticking. "Hmmmm, this needs some work too." He began to take apart the lock. In about twenty minutes he put it all back together and cleaned up his mess. "Lookin' good. Should have fixed this lock ages ago." He jotted in his notebook, "Toilet seat and door lock."

Earnest was again working on the garage door when Sonny skipped out of the house, singing to himself. He pulled his hanky out of his pocket and waved it at Earnest as he drew near.

"Let's call a truce," he said hopefully. "I wanna go fishing before it rains and before our spring break is all used up."

Earnest wiped sweat from his tired brow and glanced toward the lake. "Okay. I could use a break. Just keep that nose-wiper out o' my face."

The boys collected their fishing gear and started across the lawn. Before they got to the edge of the highway, their father called to them. "Hey! You guys know anything about this mower?"

Sonny and Earnest turned around and scurried back. They set down their fishing rods. "What's wrong?" Sonny asked.

Mr. Wheeler motioned toward the grass. "Look at this lawn. If I don't get it mowed today, I'll need a chain saw to cut it. It's supposed to rain again tonight, and this mower is deader than last year's Christmas tree."

Sonny stooped down and ran his face all over the mower, like dog sniffing a dead rabbit. "Is it getting gas?"

"I'm sure of it. Filled the tank, too. The line seems to be open. You can smell it coming through."

"Spark?" Sonny asked next.

"I put in a new plug."

Sonny scratched his head. "I don't get it. Everything looks right. It was working fine last week."

Earnest stepped forward with a smug look. "Let me take a look at it." He turned the mower around and probed around it with his finger. Then as if by magic he put his finger on the problem. "Hey! Here we go. This coil wire is loose, see?" He pulled a penny from his pocket and tightened the little screw head. "Now try it."

Mr. Wheeler flipped the switch and primed the gas. When he pulled the cord the machine exploded to life. He grinned, waved a thank you to the boys, and shoved off across the lawn.

Sonny hung his head in defeat. His mouth hung open and his eyes were glazed. "Why do I get the feeling I'm losing this contest all over the place?"

Earnest smiled and shrugged. He scribbled in his notebook, "Fixed power mower."

The boys grabbed their rods and raced across the highway to Long Branch Lake.

It was almost supper time when they came dragging back across the highway. Mr. Wheeler had mowed the lawn and was almost done trimming the hedges.

"You boys look defeated."

"Yeah," Sonny replied. "The water was real muddy from all this rain. All we caught were little catfish and crawdads."

"Well, your mother will have a good meal for us. That will lift your spirits. She should have it on the table by the time we get cleaned up." He glanced at his watch.

When the three of them tramped into the kitchen, the kitchen was dark and empty.

Mr. Wheeler stopped and looked around with a question mark on his face. "What's going on here? Did your mother say anything to you about eating out tonight?"

The boys shook their heads.

A muffled voice called from down the hall. "Ralph? Ralph, is that you? Ralph?"

The three of them followed the sounds to the bathroom, where they stood listening.

"Get me outta here, Ralph!"

Mr. Wheeler unfastened the door lock and opened the door. There stood Mrs. Wheeler, her face scarlet and her blonde hair hanging wet and wild.

She crossed her arms and glared at the boys. With the voice of a hungry animal she growled, "WHO MESSED WITH THIS LOCK?"

Sonny meekly held up one finger.

"Well, you might like to know you got it on backwards! I have spent the entire afternoon in this stupid, smelly, dinky little room. I have yelled! I have screamed! I have beaten on this door till my hands were bloody! I have cried. I have prayed. I have taken a shower. I washed my hair. I trimmed my nails. I cleaned the cabinets. I broke the mirror with my shoe! I have read six back issues of *Good Housekeeping* magazine!" Sonny glanced at Earnest, and Earnest was studying his father's face.

Mrs. Wheeler went on. "I can tell you how many squares of tile are on the walls. I have worn a groove in the floor from pacing back and forth." She was beginning to run down, but her face was still throbbing with anger.

Suddenly she whirled and stomped away toward the bedroom. She stopped and glared back. "I will expect my supper to be served in bed, and it had better be a *dandy!*"

No one said anything for several seconds. Then Mr. Wheeler shook his head and smiled. "Sonny, I guess this just isn't your day. 'Spect we better make a quick trip to a fine restaurant if we want to go on living in this house."

Earnest held his hand to his mouth to hide his smile.

8 • In Pain

On Friday morning, a truck squeaked to a standstill in the Wheelers' driveway. Sonny pulled back the kitchen curtain and peered out. "Somebody here from Mulkey's furniture."

Ralph Wheeler jumped up from the breakfast table, his face all aglow. "That must be the new bed I ordered."

Mrs. Wheeler frowned. "Ralph! You ordered a new bed? A whole new bed?"

"Sure did. A king-sized job, too."

For the next few minutes Mr. Wheeler and the

delivery man weaved in and out of the house with bed parts.

"Look out, mattress coming through."

"Watch the lamp, Ralph."

"Here's the bolts."

"Will it fit in the room? It's huge!"

At last the new bed was all set up. Mr. Wheeler signed the bill, then went to the bedroom to admire the new purchase. Sonny and Earnest were bouncing up and down on the new mattress like porpoises in water.

"What a boring bed," Earnest said. "No squeaks at all."

Sonny flattened out on the mattress and sniffed it. "Smells like flowers. Cherry would love it."

Mrs. Wheeler stroked the mattress, then stood back to admire it. "I just hope we can pay for it, Ralph."

"Well," he replied, "it was a little expensive, but if we get twenty years out of it, that's only about $50 a year. When you figure you spend one-third of your life in bed, it's worth it. I feel sleepy just looking at it."

"A third of your life?" Earnest asked. "I'll bet Sonny spends more like half of his life in bed."

The Wheelers went back to work. Sonny

yawned as he looked at his long list of things to do. "I think I need a jump start." He shuffled outdoors where Cherry had left a wagonload of broken toys the neighbor kids had donated to the contest.

Earnest checked the windows to make sure everyone had left the house. Then he grabbed a screwdriver and tiptoed to the living room. He looked all around, then grabbed the TV and twisted the heavy thing sideways so he could get behind it. Quickly he unfastened the cable wire and refastened it to the wrong screws. Breathing hard, he twisted the TV back the way it was, then dusted his hands and left the house. He didn't notice Cherry watching him through the door window as she picked a bouquet of flowers. And on the floor lay the screwdriver he forgot to put back.

"Hey, Earnest!" Sonny hollered from the garage. "Look at this!"

Earnest turned and spotted Sonny jumping up and down on the old mattress that was sitting beside the garage. A big grin came to his face. He ran toward Sonny, leaped into the air, and bounced on the mattress. For several minutes the boys bobbed up and down on the homemade trampoline.

When they stopped to rest, Earnest squinted at

Sonny's eye and said, "Are you sure your eye is okay? It looks funny."

Sonny bounded off the mattress and took off for the kitchen. "Leave my eye alone. I'm gonna fix the kitchen door."

Cherry suddenly rounded the corner of the house with a fistful of lilacs. She tapped on the office door, then stepped inside.

Mrs. Wheeler was on the phone. She smiled at the sight of the flowers, and handed Cherry a styrofoam cup to use as a vase. At last she hung up the phone.

"The lilacs are lovely, Cherry. The whole yard is just beautiful. Ralph was just saying how nice it looks, and he never even pays attention to such things."

Cherry blinked and rubbed the soles of her sandals together. With a whispery voice she thanked Mrs. Wheeler, then added, "Can I ask you something?"

Mrs. Wheeler nodded. "Sure."

Cherry wrinkled her brow and stared at the floor. The room was silent for a few seconds. At last she got up her courage. "Mrs. Wheeler, what should you do when you know somebody is doing something wrong and you want to stop them but you like the somebody and you don't want to hurt him . . . or her."

"Hmmmmmm. Who is this mystery person?"

Cherry shrugged. "I can't tell you."

"I see. Well, it's pretty hard to beat the Golden Rule. You know, 'Do unto others as you would have them do unto you.'"

Cherry scratched her arm. "But I don't understand."

"Well, Cherish, if you were doing something bad, what would you want people to do to you?"

"I guess I would want them to stop me. But I would be so embarrassed I would just die." She twisted a strand of her red hair tighter and tighter and bit her lip harder and harder.

Mrs. Wheeler said nothing for a while, giving her time to think. Then she added, "Which is worse, Cherish, to feel embarrassed or to feel guilty?"

Suddenly the conversation was interrupted by a long, piercing scream. Then another, and a third one even worse than the others.

"That's Sonny!" Cherry said, jumping up.

"You're right! He must be hurt. C'mon."

The two of them dashed out the door and looked all around. Then they spotted Sonny, lying on the porch floor, moaning and writhing in pain.

Mrs. Wheeler was first up the porch steps, followed by Cherry, then Earnest.

Sonny was clutching his hands to his chest.

"Sonny! What's wrong?" Mrs. Wheeler touched him carefully.

Sonny went on moaning and rolling on the floor. Mrs. Wheeler knelt over him and examined him for problems. Tears drained from his eyes and his frame quivered like someone freezing. Finally he held out his shaking hands for his mother to see.

"Oh, Sonny! How did you do this?" His fingertips were smashed and purple, with flecks of red oozing out from under his nails.

Sonny moaned, trying to find the strength to talk. "I was fixing this door. . . . And I had my fingers in the hinge crack and the wind blew the door shut. Ohhhhhhhh."

"Oh, Sonny, no! My poor, poor Sonny." She cupped his hands in hers and studied them. "I don't think anything is broken, but this will be a long time healing. I'm so sorry."

Cherry had tears in her eyes and she kept playing with her own fingers. But Earnest looked at Sonny and sneered. "Crybaby, crybaby." He

sounded happy. "Now I *know* I'm going to win this contest," he added. "How can I lose against a crybaby cripple?"

He turned and started down the porch steps, but Mrs. Wheeler grabbed him by the back of his slacks. He jolted to a halt, and his mother spun him around with a violent jerk. She pointed a long finger at him.

"*You* go sit in the garage and wait for me!" She grabbed him by the wrist, bent it behind his back in a hammerlock, and propelled him toward the garage. Earnest stumbled, looked back once, then did as he was told. Mrs. Wheeler turned back to Sonny.

Sonny sat up. Soon his moans began to get

shorter and softer. The tears continued to leak down his face and he licked them as they went by his lips.

In a few minutes he was in the house, lying in his bed and chewing aspirin gum for his pain.

When he began to feel a little better, he said, "Mom, I'm sorry about the tears. I didn't mean to be a baby."

She looked surprised. "Crying isn't just for babies, Sonny. Everybody cries. It just means you are alive, that's all." She paused a minute and added, "You know, your father cried when you were born. There were problems. We thought you might not make it for a while."

"Dad cried?"

"Sure, Many times."

Sonny looked away. "But it's not just my fingers I was crying about."

"Oh?"

He nodded. "It's the contest. I don't have a chance to win now. How am I gonna fix anything with my hands like this?"

"Well, just extend the contest a few weeks longer."

Sonny wrinkled his mouth. "No way. It's in the contract. The contest is over *tomorrow noon*.

Earnest would never change it. It might as well be written in rock."

Mrs. Wheeler shrugged her shoulders. "Well, you certainly deserve to win after the way your brother acted." She stood up to leave. "But you boys will have to work that out yourselves." She left and went outside.

Earnest was sitting on a box in the garage office when his mother wrenched open the door and stormed inside.

Mrs. Wheeler paced back and forth, trying to collect her thoughts. She held a ruler, shifting it from hand to hand like a knife thrower warming up. Earnest kept a sharp eye on the ruler and sat very still and quiet.

At last she found her voice. She shook the ruler in his face as she began to speak, and Earnest shrank back. "Earnest, you are a big, big disappointment to me." She wrung the ruler in her strong, slender hands. "If you weren't too big to paddle, why, so help me . . ." The ruler snapped in her hands and she pitched it wildly at a wastebasket. Earnest winced and held his breath.

His mother went on. "I have never seen anything so rude, so thoughtless, so . . . so downright . . . *ugly*."

Earnest tried to look innocent.

"And don't you sit there and pretend you don't know what I'm talking about." She took a deep breath and went on. "Your poor brother was lying up there on the porch *suffering*. And you were laughing at him and calling him names. *How could you?* Don't you have any feelings at all?"

Earnest dropped his head and played with his thumbs.

For a long time Mrs. Wheeler said nothing, trying to gain her composure. She sat down on a wooden box and crossed her arms. "Earnest, that is truly low, calling your brother a 'crybaby cripple.' Just plain scummy."

"I'm sorry," Earnest mumbled. "I just didn't think. I didn't mean it that way."

His mother slowed her breathing and uncrossed her arms. She brushed the hair out of her eyes and leaned forward, pleading with him. "Earnest, somewhere in the Bible I read that if you laugh when your enemy falls, God will see it and not be happy with you."

"I said I was sorry, Mom. What do I have to do, crawl on my hands and knees?"

They sat in silence for a while, then Earnest dared to get up. He moseyed out into the shop, and his mother went back into the house.

Sonny got up from the bed. Holding his hands up and out of the way, he strolled outdoors. With his foot he pried open the door of his old car and plopped down on the seat to think. Suddenly the other door opened and Earnest climbed in and sat down in the passenger's seat. He cleared his throat and stared out the window blankly.

"Sorry about what I said," he mumbled. "I didn't mean it like it came out. Know what I mean?"

Sonny sighed. "Don't worry about it. It bothered Mom more than me. I'm used to living with a jerk."

Earnest grinned. "But this doesn't mean I'm gonna coast on in. A contest is a contest, and I plan to beat you like always."

Sonny nodded. He held his smashed fingers in front of his face. "I just wish somebody could fix fingers as easy as broken lamps and faucets."

9 • In Deep Water

Cherry shuffled down the driveway, heading for home, when Mrs. Wheeler hollered after her. "Cherry! Why don't you stay for supper?"

Cherry paused, and her face beamed. She skipped back to the house and bounced up the porch steps.

"We're having fried chicken," Mrs. Wheeler explained, "and I know how much you like it."

Cherry squealed and clapped. "I'll have to call my grandma and tell her where I am." She reached for the kitchen phone.

Sonny held his chicken leg with his palms because his fingers were all bandaged. "I feel like a leper," he said, rolling his eyes.

Earnest whispered to Cherry and Cherry began to giggle. She looked at Sonny and asked, "What's wrong with your eye?"

"For pity's sake, there's nothing wrong with my eye, I keep telling you guys." He glared at Earnest. "What did he tell you?"

Cherry looked flustered. "He said you glued your eye shut."

Sonny leaped up and put his wrists on his hips. He fired a mean look at his mother and shouted. "Mom! You promised not to tell! You *promised!*"

"Sit down, Sonny," Earnest said. "She didn't tell me anything. *You* did. I heard you screaming for help. People in Australia probably heard you screaming."

Sonny sat down with a thump. "Then you knew all along?"

Earnest smiled a smug smile.

Sonny pointed a bandaged hand at Earnest and said, "I'll get you for this, Earnest. Believe me, I will."

Mr. Wheeler stood up and glanced at his watch. "Well, guess I'll catch the evening news." Glancing out the window, he shook his head. "Raining again. Maybe you guys ought to build us an ark."

Cherry, Earnest, and Sonny lingered at the table for strawberries and ice cream. While they slurped and babbled, the rain began to pour down heavier and faster until they could hardly hear themselves talk.

All at once Mr. Wheeler turned the TV up very loud and slapped the side of it.

"Sonny! Earnest!" he yelled from the living room. The boys raced to his side, Cherry traipsing along behind.

"What's wrong with this TV? They are giving emergency weather warnings, but I can't hear what they're saying." He peered behind the set. "What's this screwdriver doing here? Has somebody been messin' with this set? I'm gonna mess with somebody's brain if they have."

Cherry locked eyes with Earnest. Earnest turned pale. He blinked, trying to look innocent, but his face was green with guilt.

"Maybe I can fix it," he said. Quickly he wriggled behind the set and put the wires back where they belonged. Instantly the picture cleared up.

"Flash flood warnings," the newscaster was saying. "We've had six inches of rain in three days, and we could get up to five more inches during the night if it continues at this rate. . . ."

Mr. Wheeler turned down the volume and looked around at the family with worried eyes. His mustache seemed to be quivering. "This could be a real problem," he said sternly. "Sonny, Earnest, get an umbrella and check the windows on all the cars in the lot, then check the garage windows. Then go in the garage and get anything up off the floor that might be ruined by water." He turned to his wife. "Joyce, check the basement. Make sure the sump pump is working. That basement leaks like a sieve." He peered out the window and saw that the sky was as dark as bedtime. "I'm gonna move some cars out of that low area or they may get flooded." He reached in the closet for his raincoat, then rushed out the side door.

Sonny and Earnest fought over the only umbrella, then Sonny gave up and plopped a plastic bowl on his head as he ran through the kitchen.

Mrs. Wheeler and Cherry struggled to unlatch the basement door. Cherry flipped on a light switch and Mrs. Wheeler started down the narrow, rickety steps. Halfway down she stopped with a yelp. "Cherry! Go get Ralph and the boys, quick! We've got problems."

Cherry stumbled up the steps, raced to the kitchen door and stared out into the dark rain. "Mr. Wheeler," she screamed, but her small voice was swallowed up by the noisy rain. She screamed again, but still Mr. Wheeler just sloshed along through the car lot with his back to her.

Cherry pranced around with a look of panic in her eyes. Then she grabbed the porch light switch and began flipping it on and off rapidly.

At last Mr. Wheeler stopped and turned around and looked back at the house. In a moment he came crashing through the puddles and up to the porch steps.

"What's wrong?" he gasped, out of breath.

Cherry's eyes were as big as quarters. She pointed to the basement door. "The basement. It's *flooded.*"

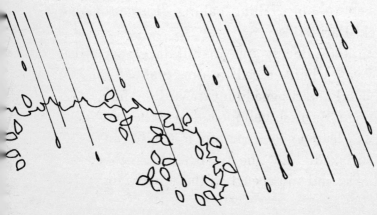

Mr. Wheeler pointed himself toward the basement. His big boots squeaked and splashed and sloshed across the carpet. He peered down the basement steps and saw his wife trying to fill a bucket with the murky, greasy water that filled the basement six inches deep.

He clomped down the steps. "Oh, no! The pump isn't working! My power tools. Get my tools up on the work bench. Get those wires up. No, wait! Don't touch those wires." He pulled on his rubber gloves and moved the wires. Then he began to work on the sump pump.

Cherry tore back up the stairs. She raced to the kitchen and ripped open the door. Out into the rain she staggered, screaming, "Earnest! Earnest! Earnest!" In moments her dress was soaked and her sandals disappeared in the deep puddles. Still she kept running, falling, calling. "Earnest! Come quick! Earnest!"

Earnest suddenly appeared in the garage office doorway. Cherry raced to him, grabbed him by the hand and dragged him toward the house.

When Earnest galloped down the basement steps he let out a long, painful moan. "I can fix it," he shrieked. "Let me fix it!" He grabbed his father's hand and peeled off the rubber gloves. He pulled them on to his own hands, then began to fiddle with the black motor of the sump pump. Mr. Wheeler watched his son intently, wondering if he could help or if he should take charge himself. "We've got to get this thing working," he yelled above the rain. If we don't, we'll lose the furnace motor, the washer and dryer, maybe even the water heater." He turned and moved a big wooden box up to the top of the workbench.

With a humming, sloshing, slurping sound the sump pump came to life.

"All right! You got it going!" Mr. Wheeler shouted. He hugged Earnest and added, "Son, I never knew you were so good at fixing things."

For a long time the water still rose, but gradually it began to go down as the pump did its job. Sonny arrived in time to find the family carrying buckets of water up the steps, where they poured them out the side door. He stood by helpless, his bandaged hands wet and dripping. At last the concrete floor became visible under a thin layer of water.

A few minutes later the family gathered in the kitchen to rest. "Look at us," Sonny blurted out. "We're a mess! A total mess!"

Mr. Wheeler shook his head. "I hate to think

where we would be without Earnest. He saved the day. I mean the *night*." He ruffled Earnest's hair, but Earnest wasn't smiling. He dropped his head, then noticed Cherry looking at him with eyes that seemed to go right through him. He stared at his muddy shoes.

"Oh, look how humble he is," Sonny teased, but Earnest did not smile. Slowly he got to his feet and shuffled off to his room.

"Well," Sonny mumbled to himself. "I guess I lost my encyclopedias. Oh, well, I never read them anyway. I was going to give them to him until he started showing off."

Cherry looked at his bandaged hands, then stared into his eyes. "Maybe you give up too easy," she said. "The contest isn't over until tomorrow, you know."

Sonny nodded and tried to smile, but nothing happened.

10 • The Truth

On Saturday morning the Wheeler used car lot looked like a lake covered with boats instead of a car lot. The water was going down only slowly.

Mr. Wheeler and Sonny were working on the garage door, but with no luck. Earnest sat quietly on the porch steps, just thinking deeply. He rolled a little ball of mud back and forth with his foot. Then he smashed it. Then he rolled it around again. Over and over he rolled and smashed the ball, as if he was smashing something deep inside himself.

Cherry was suddenly there, beside him, like a ghost out of nowhere.

"Yo! Don't sneak up on me like that," he said.

She sat beside him on the steps and said nothing.

"What's up?" Earnest finally asked. "It's not like you to have nothing to say. Are you all right?"

She smoothed her yellow sun dress and looked up at him smartly. Her eyes seemed to look right into his soul. "I know what you have been doing, and it's not fair."

"What are you talking about, Cherry?" He had a silly smirk on his face, and his foot stopped playing with the mud ball.

"I know how you've been winning the contest. You've been *breaking* things. That way you know exactly how to fix 'em. You know just what's wrong because you broke it."

Earnest looked off into the distance. "That's ridiculous. You could never prove it. Who would believe you?"

"I *saw* you," Cherry went on. "I saw you messing up that pump thing in the basement, and the TV . . . and the lawn mower."

Earnest winced. He said nothing, but his face was drooping with guilt.

"And I'm gonna tell," Cherry added, nailing her case down solid.

Earnest grabbed her by the arm. "NO! I mean, *please, no.*"

"But you tricked him. It's not fair. Everybody thinks you are real smart, and real . . . good, but you're just a cheat, that's all. Just a bad cheat."

"Okay, okay. Maybe I fudged a little." Earnest stared off in the distance. His voice turned sad and he added, "I'll withdraw from the contest, but only if you promise not to tell."

Cherry thought about it a moment. "You mean you'll let Sonny win?"

Earnest nodded. Cherry seemed to calm down. Her face lost its angry tones and took on a look of self-hate.

"Okay," she said softly. "Then I won't tell. But I should, 'cause you didn't play fair."

Cherry seemed satisfied with the promise. She got up and snaked her way through the puddles to where Sonny and his father were working on the garage door. Up and down they worked the door, but it never went higher than halfway. Cherry watched them in silence, playing with a strand of her red hair.

"What's this piece for?" she asked. She touched

a small piece of wire that stuck out into the metal door track.

"Where?" Sonny asked. He had to stoop down beside her in order to see the tiny piece of wire. "It looks to me," Cherry added, "that it's in the way of this little wheel thing."

Sonny nodded. "Yeah, it does look like that." He halfheartedly bent the wire out of the way with his only finger that wasn't smashed. Before he could take another breath, the door moved all the way to the top with a swish and a hum.

Sonny's mouth fell open. "The door! It's working! She fixed the stupid door!" He grabbed Cherry and squeezed her. "What a lady! She just charmed this door right up the track. Whooo!"

Mr. Wheeler pulled out his billfold and fingered two twenties and a ten. He folded them and planted them firmly in Cherry's little palm.

"What's this?" she asked with wide eyes full of wonder.

"It's yours," Mr. Wheeler said cheerfully. "I promised fifty dollars to anyone who could fix the door. Go on, take it, keep it."

Cherry held the crisp bills up to her face. In her small fingers the bills looked like a million dollars. "Wow," she whispered to herself. "I'm rich." She flashed a shy smile at the boys, then looked up into Mr. Wheeler's face like a puppy who had just been fed. "Thanks, Mr. Wheeler. Are you sure this is all mine?"

He nodded. "You bet. And it's *you* we should thank. Not only did you fix the door, but you have made this whole yard look like a park." He waved his hand toward the shrubs. "Just look at this place. It's a showcase!"

Cherry blushed, but there was a tiny spark of pride in her eyes. She folded the bills and wriggled them into her dress pocket. Then she turned and skipped down the drive for home.

Earnest waited until his father was gone. Then he shuffled over to Sonny, who was making the garage door go up and down over and over again.

"Sonny," he began, in a soft but determined voice. "I think I'm going to drop out of this contest."

Sonny blinked twice. "Say what?"

"I said I'm dropping out." He had a smug look on his face. "It's not a challenge anymore. I mean, I'm way ahead of you, and . . ."

Sonny frowned. "So? I don't want your pity."

"Don't worry," Earnest assured him. "No pity from me. It's just that I'm not having fun, so why

go on? I read a book and fix something, and that's all there is to it."

Sonny's face was a puzzle. He scratched his head. "Earnest, I will never understand you. And I've never known you to give up on anything."

Earnest shrugged. "First time for everything."

Sonny looked at him with suspicion. "Wait a minute! Your computer is broken, right? Is that it?"

"Nope. Computer's fine. It's yours for a month." He turned and walked rapidly toward the house. His eyes were full of moisture.

Sonny just stood watching him, dumbfounded.

Earnest moped into the house and shuffled down the hall to his room. He slammed the bedroom door behind him and locked it. For a while he stood there quietly, unable to decide whether to cry or get angry. Then he grabbed a coat hanger off the bed and began to bend it out of shape.

"I lost the stupid contest! I lost the fifty dollars! To a ten-year-old! I lost *everything!*"

The coat hanger was now a twisted mess. He leaned back and heaved the wire pretzel at the wall. It ripped a poster, bounced on to the stereo, then sprang back, landing at his feet like a boomerang.

With a growl he flung himself on his bed and beat the mattress with his fists. Then he grabbed his pillow and chewed on it like a mad dog.

At last his self-hate was spent. He lay very still and breathed slow and long.

And then the tears came.

After lunch, Sonny headed straight for Earnest's room. Earnest and Cherry trailed right behind him.

"Ha ha! Can't wait to get my hands on this computer," Sonny said.

Earnest perched on the edge of his bed and watched Sonny closely, like a detective, lest he hurt the machine.

"Where do you keep your disks?" Sonny asked eagerly.

"Disks? The contract didn't say anything about disks. Just the computer."

Sonny leaped up. "Oh, come on! Don't try to be cute! Where's the disks, come on, cough up."

Cherry glared at Earnest as if to say, "Be fair, or I'll tell on you."

Earnest signed and pointed to a drawer. "In there, but if you break anything, I'm telling you I'll never forgive you."

Soon Sonny was tapping away at the keyboard

with his good finger. His face seemed electrified and he hummed happily to himself as he worked.

Earnest stared at the wall, too nervous to watch. Suddenly he stiffened. "Hey, where did these books come from? What are they doing on my shelf?"

Sonny glanced over his shoulder. "Oh, those? I put them there."

"But those are your encyclopedias. The ones I was trying to win."

Sonny smiled. "I know, I'm giving them to you."

"Giving them?"

Sonny kept working at the keyboard. "Sure, why not? I never use 'em. Besides, I need the space for my hubcap collection."

Earnest just stared unbelieving at his brother. Then he glanced at Cherry. She just shrugged and smiled back.

Earnest thumbed through the books for a few moments and sniffed them. Then he reached for a chair and pulled it up beside Sonny. He put one arm around his brother, and with the other hand he pointed to the keyboard.

"Here, Sonny. Let me show you what this baby can do."

Wheeler's Adventures

Wheeler's Big Break
Sonny and Earnest have a contest to see which one can fix the most broken items in one week.

Wheeler's Vacation
On a vacation to California, Earnest sets out to prove that he doesn't have to have fun if he doesn't want to.

Wheeler's Freedom
Sonny and Earnest are left home to take care of themselves for a whole week.

Wheeler's Campaign
The brothers agree to manage each other's campaigns for class president.